How do I use this scheme?

Key Words with Peter and Jane has three
parallel series, each containing twelve books. All three
series are written using the same carefully controlled
vocabulary. Readers will get the most from **Key Words** with
Peter and Jane when they follow the reading pattern
1a, 1b, 1c; 2

gradually

provides further   of these same words, but
in a different context and with different illustrations.

• Series c

uses familiar words to teach **phonics** in a methodical way,
enabling children to read increasingly difficult words.
It also provides a link to writing.

Published by Ladybird Books Ltd
A Penguin Company
Penguin Books Ltd., 80 Strand, London WC2R 0RL, UK
Penguin Books Australia Ltd, 707 Collins Street, Melbourne, Victoria 3008, Australia
Penguin Group (NZ) 67 Apollo Drive, Rosedale, North Shore 0632, New Zealand

022

ISBN: 978-1-40930-145-5

Printed in China

Key Words

with Peter and Jane

9b Jump from the sky

written by W. Murray
illustrated by M. Aitchison

Peter and Jane have an uncle who can fly an aeroplane. The two children are with this uncle today. They are at an Aeroplane Show. Many people have come to see the aeroplanes.

They put their car in the car park and walk over to where the aeroplanes are on show. The sky is blue and the sun is out.

"I'm glad it's fine weather," says Jane to her uncle.

"Yes," he says, "it's just the day we want for the show."

As they walk round, Uncle tells Peter and Jane about the aeroplanes. He knows a lot about them and he has been up in some of them.

"It makes me want to learn to fly," says Peter. "I've never been up in an aeroplane."

"I'll take you up one day," says his uncle. "Would you like to come, Jane?" he asks.

"Of course," says Jane. "I want to go up as soon as I can."

Then Uncle tells the children that he is going up to jump from an aeroplane.

Uncle has left Peter and Jane, as he has to go up in his aeroplane with some more men and then jump out. It is part of the show.

Peter and Jane go back to the car park and wait to see their uncle come down. They look up into the sky and talk to each other as they wait.

"I hope he won't be in danger," says Jane.

"I hope not," says Peter. "Uncle knows what to do, of course. He's been doing it for a long time."

All the people watch the aeroplane climb up and up. Soon it is so far up that it looks very small.

Up in the aeroplane Uncle and the other men look down. They can see a long way as it is a fine day. The people and the buildings look very small to them. They talk about the jump they are going to make. They will take turns to jump out of the aeroplane.

The men in the aeroplane are ready to jump
out. They enjoy doing this, and they know that
many people enjoy this part of the show more
than any other.

One of the men jumps. He falls quickly at first
and then more slowly. Now it is Uncle's turn.
He jumps out of the aeroplane and falls very
quickly. Then he goes down more slowly.

All the other men throw themselves out in turn. Soon they all come down together. The people can see them against the blue sky as they fall. It takes some time, and many people with cameras take photographs.

The children watch from the car park and then walk to the aeroplanes again. They are going to tell their uncle they are glad all went well.

"I enjoy it when Uncle jumps, but I'm glad when it's over," says Jane.

"I know what you mean," says Peter. "I would like to go up in an aeroplane but I wouldn't like to jump out."

9

Uncle is with Peter and Jane again. "I think you like jumping like that," says Jane.

"Yes, you enjoy it, don't you?" asks Peter.

Uncle says, "Yes, I enjoy doing it. Now we'll do something you like. What do you want to do?"

"Let's go over there, by that small building," says Peter. "Anyone can buy a balloon there. The man will blow it up. Then you can write your name and where you live on the balloon."

"Why do you have to do that?" asks Jane.

Peter says, "You do it only if you want to. You let the balloon go up into the sky. It may come down far away. If someone finds it he may send it back to you from a long way away."

They find Bob and Mary together over by the balloons. There are other children there. One father has a camera. He takes a photograph of his children by the pretty balloons.

Peter, Jane and their two friends each want to buy a balloon.

The children like to look at the colours of the balloons and to watch the man blowing them up for other children. Then they each pick the colours they want for themselves. Peter has a white balloon, Bob a red one, Mary a pretty blue one and Jane a pretty yellow one.

They give the man their money for the balloons and he blows them up. Then they write their names on the balloons and are ready to send them off.

First Bob holds up his arm with his red balloon in his hand and lets it go. It goes up at once and they all watch it. Then Peter sends off his white balloon in the same way. The two girls have their turn next. They hold up their arms together and let their balloons fly off at the same time.

"It's like a race," says Jane.

"Yes, a balloon race," says Mary.

"I hope they all go a long way and that someone sends them back to us," says Bob.

13

It is the day after the Aeroplane Show. It is another fine day. The sun is out and the sky is blue again. Here is a man on a farm some way away from the home of Peter and Jane.

The man has been at work all the morning and now he is going home for his dinner. He stops to look at his cows as they eat the grass. He can see something white as it comes down slowly against the trees.

The man has a dog with him and it runs after the white balloon. The man calls the dog to him as it is jumping at the balloon. He does not want the dog to make the cows run away. He walks over the grass to pick up the balloon.

When he looks at it he can see the writing. He reads what it says. "I ought to send this back," he says to himself. He lets the balloon down and takes it with him.

The next day he sends it off to Peter.

15

This man is in a boat on the sea. The boat is not going along, as the man has put a rope from the boat on to some rocks, while he tries to get some fish. There are six fish in the boat and more in the water. As the man looks down into the water he can see some more fish as they swim about. The water is not very deep by the rocks.

Soon he throws two more fish into the boat. "That makes eight," he says to himself.

Then the man looks up into the sky. As he looks up he sees something round and red. It is the red balloon, and it comes down into the boat on to some rope.

The man turns round to pick up the balloon. He picks it up to throw it into the water. As he does this he sees the writing and stops. He reads the writing and then puts the balloon back into the boat.

It is a warm sunny afternoon, just the weather to play outside. Here are some men having a game of cricket. They all have white cricket clothes. The two men with the bats play very well, and they are making a lot of runs. The other men can't get them out. Again and again the big man in the white cap hits the ball away. Sometimes he hits a six.

Many people are here. It is nice to sit outside in the warm sun and watch the cricket. They like to see the big man hit out at the ball, as it is making the game more interesting.

Then something makes the people laugh. The men who play the game laugh, too. Just as the man is about to hit the ball a yellow balloon comes down by his face. He can't see the ball as he tries to hit it.

Another man picks up the balloon and takes it away. He gives it to a small boy who has come to watch the game.

This is the man who looks after the town clock. He has to see that it keeps good time. He looks after the inside and also the outside of the clock. Sometimes he has to paint its face.

Today he has made the clock stop. The big hand is on the six and the little hand is by the eight. He is going to paint the face and hands. He has the paint ready.

The man can look down into the street from where he is. He sees the town people going to work. Many of them walk, and others go by bus or car. Some of them look up at the clock, but today it does not tell the right time.

Then some children go by on their way to school. They look up at the man at work on the clock and stop and laugh. They can see a blue balloon blowing along by the clock face. The man throws the balloon down to the children. They wait for it and then take it to school.

The two boys are having fun together in the garden with a gun and some bubbles. The girls are not here, they are inside the house. Jane and Mary are in the kitchen. They like to help Jane's mother to cook. She lets them cook in the kitchen once a week.

The gun is Peter's. It looks like a real gun but it is not a real one. It is a toy gun he bought from a shop, and it can't hurt anyone. It shoots out little white balls.

Bob is blowing bubbles. You can see colours in the bubbles he is blowing. The boys watch the bubbles go up by the trees.

"Let me shoot at the bubbles," says Peter. He gets down on the grass and shoots little white balls at the bubbles.

At first Peter can't hit any of the bubbles. Then he does. One of the balls hits Bob, but it does not hurt him. "Don't shoot at me," he says.

"You have a turn," says Peter. "You shoot and I'll blow bubbles."

It is Bob's turn to shoot. "Thank you," he says, as he takes the gun from Peter.

Peter blows some bubbles. He makes little ones at first. As he looks at them he says, "I like the colours in these bubbles. They're beautiful."

"Blow big ones," says Bob. "I can't hit little ones." Peter blows some more bubbles. After a while he makes some big ones. "Shoot at these," he says. "You can hit these."

Bob shoots. After a while he says, "I ought to hit them but I can't."

"I'll blow a very big one," says his friend. "Here you are." He blows a very big bubble.

"Look at its beautiful colours," says Bob. Then he shoots at the bubble and hits it.

"Good for you," calls out Peter. He soon blows another one.

The girls come out from the kitchen to watch the boys. They have some cakes they have made, and they give some to the boys.

"They're lovely cakes," says Bob.

"Yes, you are real cooks," says Peter.

The children have made the room dark to show pictures on the wall. The pictures are in colour and are about cowboys and cowgirls and Indians, as they looked in the old-time days.

The first one is of the cowboys at their camp. There are no Indians or cowgirls in this picture. It is night-time and it is dark, but it is not dark by the camp fire. The cowboys have been to collect wood for a big fire.

Some of the cowboys play cards, and others sing. You can just see some of their horses.

"The cowboys all have guns," says Bob.

"Yes, and we all know why," says his friend Peter. "They had guns to fight the Indians in those days."

"What did they sing about?" asks Mary.

"About many things," say the others. "About their homes, their girls, their horses and their fights with Indians."

"One cowboy is going away from the fire," says Peter. "I think he's going to collect some more wood, or to look after the horses."

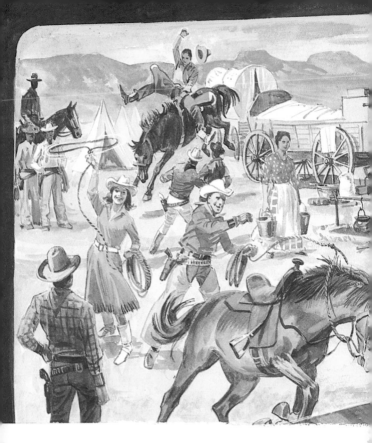

The next picture shows the cowboys' camp in the daytime. It shows cowboys and cowgirls also. Some without horses have ropes in their hands. They throw their ropes as a sport.

The children talk as they look at the picture. "The cowboys like the sport they have with their ropes and their horses," says Peter.

"I think the horses like it too. They like to run and jump," says Jane. "The ropes won't hurt them. Nobody wants to hurt a horse."

"I can throw a rope like that," says Bob. "I want to be a cowboy when I'm a man."

"I don't want to be a real cowboy," says Peter. "I just want to play cowboys and Indians now."

"Let's see some more pictures first," says Bob. "Are there any about Indians?"

"Yes," says Peter. "Some of them show the Indians' camp, and in the others you see cowboys and Indians having a fight."

"Let me show the next picture," says Bob.

"Here we are then," says Bob, as he shows another picture on the wall. "This is one of those we want to see."

It is a picture in colour of some Indians at their camp. In the picture it is night-time and the Indians have a camp fire. One of them puts some sticks on the fire and another has some more sticks ready. There are no cowboys in the picture.

"These were real Indians," says Mary. "You can see that. They are not white men who pretend to be Indians."

"They have been out to hunt," says Bob, "and now they're going to eat."

"They could hunt and fight very well," says Mary.

"The paint on their faces does not make them look very pretty," says Jane.

Peter says, "I like it. When we play, I'll pretend to be an Indian. I have some paint I can put on my face."

Bob shows the next picture. All the pictures are about cowboys and Indians and they are all in colour. The children like them very much.

There are both cowboys and Indians in this picture, but there are no cowgirls in it.

The cowboys are going through a wood on their horses. Some Indians jump out of the trees on to the cowboys. There is a fight. Some of the men fight on horses and some fall off as they fight. Some of the cowboys and Indians are hurt.

"Who will win?" asks Mary.

Bob says, "Sometimes the cowboys win and sometimes the Indians win."

"I hope the cowboys win," says Peter.

"I hope the Indians do," says Mary.

"It'll show us who wins in the next picture,"
says Jane. "I'd like to show the next one, Bob.
May I, please?"

"Yes, of course," says Bob. "You can have
your turn now."

Now it is Jane's turn. All the others watch her do it and then talk about the picture as they look at it.

This shows the end of the fight. The Indians run away to their horses. They jump up on them as quickly as they can, to get away from the cowboys. The cowboys make their own horses run after the Indians. They fire their guns as they go along.

"I said the cowboys would win," says Bob.

"Yes," says Peter. "They did that time."

"I hope that someone looked after the cowboys and Indians hurt in the fight," says Jane.

"But there weren't many hospitals in those days," says Bob.

"That's the last of the pictures we have to show," says Peter. "What do you want to do now?"

"Let's play Cowboys and Indians," says Bob.

35

The children play Cowboys and Indians. Peter and Mary go off into the woods to get ready while Bob and Jane make a camp.

Then Peter and Mary come back. Peter

pretends to be an Indian. He has put on Indian clothes and has paint on his face and hands. He has a gun. Mary has made herself up to be an

Indian girl. They hide in the long grass and come along slowly through it, so that the cowboys will not see them.

Bob is in cowboy clothes and Jane has made herself look like a cowgirl. They are in their camp. Bob the cowboy uses his rope. He shows Jane the cowgirl how to throw it.

Then Jane says, "What's that over there in the long grass?"

Bob looks and calls out, "Indians! Get ready to fight!"

The Indians jump up and run into the cowboys' camp. The cowboys and Indians pretend to fight. They fire their guns. Then they all run off into the woods.

Two friends of Peter and Jane are out for a walk in the woods and come to an empty house. Nobody has lived in it for a long time. The boys have never seen the old building before. "Look at the roof," says one boy. "There's grass on it."

As it is raining they go into the house for a while. Then they explore the rooms. One of them falls over a piece of wood on the floor. He is hurt and can't get up.

His friend tries to help him and then goes off to tell their mothers and fathers. A doctor comes to the house to see the boy who is hurt. He looks at him for some time and then says, "You must go to hospital. I'll take you there."

Off they go to the hospital. The doctor tells the boy who is hurt that he can't go home for a while. The doctor says that the boy should be out of hospital in about three weeks.

Peter and Jane go to the hospital to see their friend who was hurt. They take him some fruit and flowers. The nurse lets them talk to their friend by his bed.

He thanks them for the fruit and the flowers and then tells them how he was hurt. "It was raining," he says, "and my friend and I went to explore an old empty house. I fell over a piece of wood on the floor in the house and I was hurt. I couldn't get up, so the doctor came. I have to be here in hospital for about three weeks, I think."

"Do you like it in here?" asks Jane.

"Yes," says their friend, "it's nice, and I like the nurses, but it's better outside. I want to run about again."

Then their friend tells them that there is a boy and a girl in the hospital who have no friends to come to see them. Their homes are a long way away.

"It would be nice to take them something," says Jane.

Peter and Jane go to the hospital again. They see their friend for a little while and give him an interesting jigsaw puzzle. They know that he likes jigsaw puzzles. Then they go to talk to the boy and girl who have no friends to see them.

Peter talks to the boy and gives him a model car and an apple. The boy likes the model car and he eats the apple. He is happy to have someone to talk to for a while.

He tells Peter he lives on a farm a long way away. Last week he fell from the roof of a barn at the farm. "My ball went up on to the roof," he said, "and I climbed up to get it."

"When I got up to the top I fell down and hurt my head. My own doctor came to our farm to see me, and then he said I would have to come to this hospital. I won't be here for more than a week."

Jane talks to the girl in bed. She gives her a book and some flowers. "Thank you," says the girl. "I like to read, and the flowers are lovely."

She tells Jane she lives by the sea and that she likes it there. Both her mother and father go out to work all day, so they can come to see her only once a week. She has no brothers or sisters.

"There aren't many houses and no hospital where I live," she says. "I had to come here to get better."

Jane tells the girl about herself. Then they talk about their schools. They both like to read. The girl reads some of the interesting book Jane gave her, to show Jane how well she can read. Then Jane reads also.

The nurse comes along to see how the girl is and she talks and laughs with the two girls. As she goes away Jane says, "What a nice nurse."

"Yes," says her new friend, "she's always like that. She makes us all happy."

45

Peter and Jane want to give some of their toys to the children in the hospital. They are by their toy cupboard. The cupboard has many toys in it. It is a big cupboard but not very deep.

"This cupboard is like a treasure house," says Peter. "We have a lot of toys. Sometimes I forget about some of them."

"Yes, it's a treasure house for toys," says Jane. "Sometimes I forget about some of our things, too."

Peter takes out his train set and then fits it back into its box. He looks at the building set, and then at the toy farm.

Jane picks up her skipping rope. She uses this skipping rope a lot. "I wish the sun would come out," she says. "I'd like to skip now." Then she puts the skipping rope down and picks up the camera. They both like taking pictures.

"It's no use taking pictures inside the house," says Peter. "We'll have to wait for the sun to come out again."

Peter fits some of the toys back into the cupboard and then sits up at the table with some cards. "Come and play a card game with me," he says to his sister.

"Let me look through this scrapbook first," says Jane. "It's fun to look at these old photographs. Here's one of Mum as she tries to skip."

Her brother comes over to look at the scrapbook. He laughs with Jane at some of the photographs. He says, "That was the day we played hide and seek after the picnic in the woods. I hid by the car, and then you hid by those logs."

"Look at Dad
in this one," says Jane.
"He has put on Mum's new hat."

"Yes," says Peter, "Mum always said it was too big for her after that. Dad had to get her another new one."

They look on through the scrapbook and then they hear someone at the door. Two of their friends have come to show them some letters they have just had.

Bob and Mary have come to see them. Mary has just had a letter about the balloon she had at the Aeroplane Show. Bob had a letter about his balloon one day last week.

Both Jane and Peter have had letters about their balloons. They go to get their letters now.

They read out their letters to each other. Mary's is from a school. The teacher has helped a little girl of six to write the letter and some of

her friends have put their names by hers at the end of it.

Jane's letter is from a boy who got her balloon at a game of cricket. He tells her how the balloon made the people laugh.

Peter's comes from a farm. "My letter says that a dog found my balloon by some cows," he says. "We can go to see the farm one day."

The last letter is Bob's. It is from a boy of eight. His father was at sea in a boat when he found the balloon. The boy wants Bob to write to him.

New words used in this book

Total number of new words: 109
Average repetition per word: 9